MYSTERIOUS

AUSTRALIA

S.T.A.R.S. Publishing

https://starsgc.com

Compilation of stories by Nerida E. Marshall

ISBN: 9780646888750

A catalogue record for this work is available from the National Library of Australia

NATIONAL LIBRARY OF AUSTRALIA

Cover design by Nerida E. Marshall
Rainbow Serpent artwork by Lee LaWeaver

In Australian indigenous mythology
Rainbow Serpent is the creator of all nature.

GHOSTS

AND

APPARITIONS

BLACK ROBED SPECTRE
Nerida Marshall

It was 1974 when I lived on the bank of the Leichhardt River in outback Mt Isa. With little warning the sky turned black and dropped a deluge of rain turning the dusty parched landscape into a lake of red mud. With a deafening crash of rocks and tree stumps a terrifying tsunami of flood water roared down the dry riverbed crushing any living thing in its path. It was that night when the blacked robed apparition first came to me. It was a spectral monk that you might expect to see when visiting the ruins of an ancient castle. A hooded figure with a large wooden cross attached to its belt of cord. But here in the glaring heat of outback Australia it was most certainly out of place. None the less it was there, walking slowing past my bedroom door. It stopped halfway to turn its head towards me. No face was visible under the hood but far from being terrified it emanated a flow of calm and wellbeing. It continued past my bedroom door and disappeared. In the morning all hell broke loose as the river roared over its banks in a churning torrent of water, trees, and dead cattle. It swept animals and people away with equal voracity. No time to panic. Just get out and move cars and pets to higher ground. Kangaroos and koalas scrambled onto car roofs while snakes and lizards clung to every bonnet. No fear now as we were all equal in the game of survival. Once on high ground every creature waited calmly for the raging waters to subside. s would overtake their high ground sanctuary. Many years later this very same implausible spectre came to me once more but in another house far away from the outback almost to the ocean. It was during a devastatingly low point in my life. It glided just the same as last time. Floating past my bedroom and stopping halfway to bathe me with a sensation of calm that the calamity of the following days would be overcome and in time the pain would heal.

NIGHT VISITOR
June Dowling

Awoken in the night
There he stood
Silhouetted in the doorway
Old man, white bushy hair and beard
Dressed like a sailor of old
A musty odour filled the room
The air chilled and made me shudder
His stern face stared at me
I sat still and just stared back
No fear I felt

Wondering from whence he came
Then in a blink of an eye
He was gone, leaving me all alone
Many times he returned
In the middle of the night
My body intuitively awoke
when the musty smell filled the air
I knew no harm he meant
He was content to stand and stare
I could only wonder why he was there

Often I called out
There came no reply
The sound of my voice
Heralded a quick good bye
He always vanished then in the blink of an eye

ELDER APPROVAL
Elizabeth Lippiatt

We bought a house. It took a year to find the right one. Our small children now had a yard to play in, a bedroom each, a cat, and the puppy they wanted. Immediately we moved in but unexpected problems arose. Over time health problems continued to arise for my husband. With his health as it was, I knew I would have to be the source of the household income.

To get a better future for us I went to university to get a degree and continued on to get a teaching qualification. Not quite through the teaching degree my own health was under threat. I had a tumour in a nearly inoperable position. It was 'tiger country' one doctor told me. Another said anything could happen and that it would be best only to have the operation if it was a matter of life and death.

One day after that in desperation to get an answer, assistance or something to get the energy of life flowing positively our way, I walked down to a corner of our block of land. I was questioning and praying for a solution to what I needed to do. I felt a strange presence and then I saw them in a hazy outline; a circle of Aboriginal Elders. Instead of fright I found I was relieved and excited. I had what I thought was a crazy idea. I asked the Elders if they would approve of my family living there and assist us with our health and safety. I waited and after a while I felt acceptance and took that for their approval. I thanked them and went back inside in a state of amazement.

After that our situation became more manageable I got myself into a position where I taught part time. That way I earned enough for us to manage while being there to assist my husband with his health issues. I needed to be around as our children were now both adolescents. Decades have now gone by. My husband passed away after a surprisingly long life for a person with so many health complications. I decided to turn my home into my own sanctuary. I planted native shrubs around the property to attract the birds. To the delight my grandchildren I placed around under the trees and shrubs statues of Australian native animals. The large garden shed with its broken concrete slab and the useless ugly concrete pathway and stairs that dissected the property, I had completely removed.

About nine months after I had done this and it was all progressing nicely I became aware of a message. It was clear and it was from the Aboriginal Elders. It was an expression of approval that I had taken away the concrete. I felt their smiles and added them to my own. Much later I wondered who's idea it was for the statues and to plant all those native shrubs. I now believe that this totally European descended person (myself) was probably far more influenced by them than I had thought.

TO BELIEVE OR NOT
Robert Young

As far as ghost stories go in Australia the state to claim the most ever is Tasmania. Starting with the first penal settlement at Port Arthur, many convicts either died or were hanged for various crimes they committed whilst serving out their time there. First set up in 1830 as a working prison and timber station, it did not take long for the stories of ghostly apparitions being seen in and around the area where the gallows were standing, waiting for their next customer to attend their appointment.

There are still reports of ghostly figures walking through the gaol and it is claimed that on Monday afternoons, the church bells can be heard ringing. By the way, the church is no longer standing. As farming grew on the island and more industries were started, the gaol remained in use until its demise in 1877. It's main claim to fame now days is it is the most haunted area in Australia. The tragic events of 1996 have only added to the carnage of the area. On April 28, Martin Bryant opened fire with an assault rifle on tourists at Port Arthur, killing 35 and wounding 21 men, women and children. Bryant was found fit to stand trial and is currently serving 35 life terms plus 1,035 years without parole in Tasmania's Risdon Prison.

Richmond Bridge, Australia's oldest bridge, in Richmond, Tasmania, is said to be haunted by the ghost of George Grover, a guard who loved whipping the convict workers a little too much and was supposedly thrown off the bridge by the convicts he tortured during its construction. No one was ever convicted of the killing. Now, the ghost of Grover walks under the bridge, seen by many drunken students and expectant tourists. The ghost of a large black and white dog, sometimes called 'Grover's Dog', is also seen on the bridge. One lady reported it by her side many times as she walked alone on the bridge at night. It would walk beside her across the structure, and then disappear once she reached solid ground. The Old Hobart Gaol is the site of many ghost tours now, yet back in the 1800s, it was the site of many executions. There are numerous stories told by the tour guides, most common are the stories of the recurring smell of blood near the gallows area, and of shadowy figures moving in the night. With buildings made from bricks manufactured by hand, and with sandstone also hewn by the hands of the convicts, a military barracks was constructed in Hobart Town in 1840 along with a military gaol attached.

Still in use today, tours are conducted only at night when the cries of those long gone can be heard – if you are game to venture there at night. Re-enactments of historical trials and the constant tours at various venues, would hardly allow the restless dead to truly rest, now would they?

THE JOKER HENRY

June Dowling

I remembered the calm and silence as I unlocked the childcare centre's door soon to be interrupted by the chatter and squeals of fifty exuberant children. I went to my room to set up for the day. First thing that caught my eye was my pile of music books that had moved to the other end of the piano. My guitar, that was usually positioned leaning in the corner beside the piano, was now situated at the other end of the room. My hat, which had been placed on top of the piano at the end of the day, now adorned the piano stool. Strange. Stranger still was to come. The toilet rolls in the children's bathroom had been removed to the washbasins and toilet brushes piled in the middle of the floor.

"Oh, for goodness sake the cleaner can't be that careless," I voiced. "I'll have a word with him."

When my assistant arrived, I asked, "Did you move my music books, hat and guitar yesterday?"

"No," she replied laughing. "The ghost must have."

Every few days items have changed places overnight but the staff and the cleaner denied responsibility.

"Must be Henry," I said and so we lovingly adopted our resident ghost. Never seen but his mischievous antics were. One night all alone as I worked tidying the storeroom I heard footsteps in the playroom. On investigation I found no one. As I turned off the light to leave, a silhouette at the bathroom door stopped me. There stood the figure of a small dark-haired man in a uniform I did not recognise. He smiled at me and vanished. I then saw the havoc he had created.

"You naughty Henry," I called out into the silence.

The next day I worked in the garden to help the children dig our new vegetable patch. What treasures we unearthed, nails, screws and long sticks of rotten timber previously belonging to sleepers.

"Where could this all have come from?" I asked one of the children's grandfather who was helping us. He was a local of the area for eighty years.

"The old railway station sat right on this spot," he answered.

"Wow," I said, "I can't believe I saw a man in the children's bathroom last night. A ghost. He had a uniform I did not recognise. I wonder if it was a station master's uniform."

"Yep, that would be Henry. Terrible, terrible accident," he stammered. "The girl he was to marry died and Henry, ten years the station master threw himself in front of the Sunday morning train. Biggest news. Front page of the paper. I remember as if it was yesterday."

"So it is Henry's ghost I saw last night. I can't believe I called him Henry as a joke," I replied.

The local replied, "Henry was always a joker. He loved kids. Wanted lots of his own. I guess that's why he stays here. It's now his happy resting place."

MAGIC

Lindy Standage

Bill mopped his wet face. Oh! This heat in Innisfail was savage and cleaning the pool was really hard work. This move from Tasmania took some getting used to for the whole family. His wife Sue and their four kids were lazing indoors with the air-con full blast.

Looking through the stunning scenery and huge flowering trees made up for a lot. Then blinking twice, out of the corner of his eye, came an unbelievable sight. An Aboriginal was standing on one leg and holding a spear but not in an aggressive way. The image was like the Stone Age people when first white people came looking for a new country, which was Australia. He just melted away, but Bill hoped to see him again.

This must be sacred ground as many stories had been told of these happenings. No good telling Sue, she wouldn't believe him, but the sighting made him feel so very special.

LOST

TREASURE

DOUBLOONS PLEASE
Elizabeth Lippiatt

"Well son, while mummy is away at work we can fix that piece of wall that she keeps on complaining about," Charlie's father organised their day together.

"That part that has that strange sticking out bit?"

"Yes, that's the bit. We didn't see it when we bought this place.

"Sneaky, hiding it didn't they dad?"

"Yes, they hid it. I did expect something as this is a very old house full of the historical elements that your mummy wanted."

"Historical elements?"

"Fancy bits. I have all the tools ready. Now we just need to pull off these three planks, tidy them up and put them back on so that they sit together as they are supposed to. Thank goodness this old house is made of proper wood it will make this job quite easy. I'll just start with this plank and then you can help me."

Charlie's father pulled one plank away then Charlie got hold of the corner of the next one and pulled. It came away surprisingly easily and Charlie landed on the floor, the plank making a clatter as it landed beside him.

"Charlie are you all right?"

"Yes, but what is that?" said Charlie as he pointed at the wall.

"Oh, there is something in there."

After a bit of effort wriggling the metal container Charlie's father managed to pull it from its hiding place in the wall.

"I wonder what this contains?" the father declared excitedly as he turned the container over slowly in his hands.

"Could it be treasure dad?" Charlie was even more excited than his father.

"It's well sealed up," Charlie's father said as he carefully shook the container. It rattled softly

"Must be a treasure dad. It must be."

Charlie hopped up and down in his excitement.

"I don't know, Charlie, let me open it. It could be anything."

"But it was hidden so it must be a valuable secret," explained Charlie.

"That is true son. I'll open it here at the kitchen table." Charlie's father carefully sliced the bindings and peeled away the tape. Prising off the lid took considerable time and effort. Success was finally achieved.

"What is it dad?" demanded Charlie as his father lifted something made of cloth out of the container. It looked to be a garment covered in a large brown stain. As the material unravelled a rather fierce looking knife rolled out, bounced on the table to land on the floor.

"Look out Charlie! Don't touch it!" Charlie's dad yelled as he dropped the garment and grabbed Charlie holding him away from the table.

"I don't like this treasure dad!"

"I don't either. I am going to have to call the police."

"Treasures are supposed to be gold doubloons and jewels dad!" Charlie's crossed arms and fierce frown expressed just how much he was unimpressed.

"I agree son. This treasure is not what it is supposed to be."

MARIANA'S EMERALD
Nerida Marshall

I jumped into the crystal green waters of the Indian Ocean. For one explosive moment my disturbance of the surface water shot silver droplets sky high. Once submerged it was eerily quiet with just the regular breaths from my scuba tank. It was an audible beat, almost a hypnotic proof of life. As I got closer to the wreck, I could hear the grinding and groaning of the timbers as the wax and wane of the current pulled her in each direction.

Once she had been a proud Spanish Galleon but now coral had almost completely covered the ancient remnants of her hull. She had been carrying untold plundered wealth from South America back to her Spanish masters. Sailing through the straight discovered by Luis Torres in 1606 between Australia and New Guinea saved weeks of valuable travel time and had an acceptable safety risk. However, the Southern hemisphere storms had not been studied and recorded long enough to realise they were heading straight into a savage tropical storm and the Mariana was destined to join her many sister Galleons impaled on the jagged reefs.

A flash of green now caught my eye. It was a large emerald on the sandy seafloor rolling back and forth with the ocean surge. Excitedly I reached out to capture my prize. But instead, disaster struck. My scuba suit sleeve was torn on the reef and blood starting pumping vigorously from a deep gash in my arm. Even for such a prize I could not risk alerting the large sharks of my injury as they hunted regularly around the reefs.

Reluctantly I headed for the surface to eventually get to a hospital for stiches and antibiotics. With my dreams now flooded with images of the huge emerald waiting for me on the ocean floor I will return to the Mariana wreck and claim my prize.

THE BEST ONE?
Robert Young

Frederick Wordsworth Ward died from a gunshot wound on 25th May, 1870. A notorious bushranger purported to have stolen twenty thousand pounds in gold and notes in his seven years plying his trade. Some historians believe he either did not steal this much, or that he spent all his treasure. Others believe the wrong man was shot and that the real bushranger lived out his life in luxury in the Roma District as a gentleman cattle or sheep breeder. Sentenced to ten years hard labour for horse stealing, he was serving out his time on Cockatoo Island in 1861 when he was granted a ticket-of-leave. He was again arrested for horse stealing and breaking his ticket-of-leave and was charged and returned to the island to serve out his original time, with a further three years added. Serving out only two, he made a bid for freedom in September 1863 with another convict, Fredrick Britton. They managed to slip their shackles and on that cold night, slipped into Sydney Harbour and despite the many sharks that frequented the area, managed to make it to shore. At just twenty-seven years old, Ward went on the run with a price of twenty five pounds on his head turning to bushranging, the only way he could manage to make a living.

Ward had a number of bushrangers who joined him, but none could match his cunning and skill. A well-educated half-caste Aboriginal girl was his one constant companion. Known as Mary Ann Bugg, her Aboriginal name was Yelliong. After a number of years of living rough in the bush whilst being hunted by the police, she bore Ward three children, finally dying of pneumonia. After her death, Ward became sullen and was heard to say that he wished his life was over. In 1870 he got his wish when he bailed up a hawker named Giovani Capasotti near Blanche's Inn at Church Gully six kilometres from Uralla. While the bushranger went to the inn, the merchant went quickly to Uralla and informed the police of the event. Arriving at the inn, a constable saw Ward testing a horse and fired a shot which spooked his horse and gave Ward time to ride off. Constable Alexander Binney who was off duty at the time, gave chase and managed to corner Ward at Kentucky Creek where a shootout followed. Ward was shot at close range, injuring him seriously, but the constable's gun was now empty, so he smashed Ward's face in with the butt of his revolver. With his death, the secret of where his treasure is hidden died with him.

Some twenty years later, a young lad searching for bird eggs, found a cave with a mouldy collection of twenty-pound notes in a bottle, believed to be some of Ward's hoard, but where the rest is remains a mystery to this day. Ward's longevity as a bushranger is put down to his excellent horse-riding ability and sheer bravado and cunning. Ward was the last of the bushrangers and the longest of any in Australia's history. Some say he was successful, but if dying in his thirties by gunshot wounds is successful, it is no wonder no one followed Thunderbolt in his chosen career.

NATURE'S

MYSTERIES

THE MESSAGE
Elizabeth Lippiatt

That white face is peeping at me.
Watching me. Seeing me.
What is it doing there as weeks ago
It's companions were gone?

I see that face each morning.
That beautiful white face.
It's still there watching me.
Perfect all on its own.

I smile at that face.
As for a time,
it's my only companion.
We both have no other.

That face is fading now,
and I ponder why it came.
It really is a mystery,
why it showed itself to me.

That single face came again, I believe,
to remind me, that each day is new.
And open, to everything beautiful,
opportunities, miraculous and wonderful.

BIRDS IN MY BACKYARD
Bev Stewart

Describing how many Australian birds visit my backyard would be difficult to estimate. Birds' behaviour of flying, squawking, singing, screeching, drinking, bathing, and breeding depends on the surroundings and what birds find attractive. On the Gold Coast, in Queensland terms, we live "on water", meaning our back yard overlooks a man-made canal of sea water. The presence of bull sharks makes most canals off limits for human swimmers. Here in my backyard, we are protected by a metal wire underwater fence between the inlet of water from the Currumbin River to our canal. Australian black swans and their yearly May to September breed of 6 or 8 cygnets, all of whom are not fond of salt water to drink, are keen for a shallow bucket of fresh drinking water with peas and corn in it. The cygnets especially love it. So do the Pacific Black Ducks that breed frequently in these waters as well as mallards. Brush turkeys are not often found in properties near the rivers or canals but more in-land. They are quiet birds but dig up quite a few gardens. Seasonal birds flying in from time to time, depending on the climate, are currawongs, sulphur-crested cockatoos, crows, cockatiels. They are attracted to our macadamia nut tree. It's a welcome difference to the cockatoos chewing away at the wooden parts of our house when we are not home. There is a 40 metre high gum tree in front of next door, which is very attractive to Australian singing birds. Magpies and butcher birds build their nests and breed their babies there every year. These are the birds which start the days' cacophony at the break of dawn much to the disgust of visitors and tourists. However, these beautiful Australian birds have musical voices. Both magpies and butcher birds swoop during spring when breeding so we wear hats. My dog, Marley, is swooped upon constantly but he thinks they've come to play chasey with him.

WEIRD AND WONDERFUL
Robert Young

Good old Aus has many weird and wonderful sights. From the morning glory cloud in the far north, to the pink lakes that stretch from Victoria's west to Western Australia. Lying approximately 130 kilometres from Esperance, Lake Hillier on Middle Island in Western Australia's Recherche Archipelago is a surreal sight. The pink lake neighbours the dark blue waters of the Indian Ocean, with a strip of lush green forest acting as a barrier. This lake as with all of them, are best seen from the air. A little further south lays another of these miracles of nature. Hutt Lagoon changes from red to pink and sometimes to purple, depending on the time of day and the time of year. The much larger Lake Eyre in South Australia is blindingly white when it is dry, but when it fills with flood waters from monsoon rains in Queensland and the Northern Territory, it looks rusty in the shallows, and changes to pink and blue as the water changes in depth.

On the Eyre Peninsular, Lake MacDonnell contrasts pink with green and blue water, with a bisque-coloured road bisecting it; a truly magnificent sight from the air. It has one of the heaviest concentrations of salt in the water in Australia, which causes these contrasts. Located in the north-west of Victoria is the Murray-Sunset National Park. The lakes here change from glistening white to beautiful pink, but they are at their best on slightly cloudy days. The change in colour here is bought about by the light and the amount of salt in the water at the time of viewing. Lake Hart in South Australia is beautiful by night or by day. This shallow pink lake has a high salt concentration that creates salt crystals under the pastel waters. Day or night, this magic wonder of nature is worth the trek to see it, as is the many other lakes that sometimes change colour as the salinity changes with the inflow of waters, from near or far in this wide and wonderfully mysterious country.

AN AUSSIE LEGEND
Lindy Standage

The legend of The Devil's Pools is still with us today.
Going back in time when many Aboriginal tribes lived in
this area, a beautiful woman named Oolana was
betrothed to the head of her tribe, then she fell deeply in
love with another, Dyga, a warrior from a different tribe.
So furious with them were her tribe that they gave chase
as Oolana and Dyga ran for their lives. Coming to a cliff
overlooking a rock pool, Dyga dived into the water but
never surfaced. Grief stricken, Oolana threw herself after
him. Suddenly the whole landscape changed as huge
boulders, trees and stones flew through the air and the
pools became raging torrents as she disappeared
beneath the turbulent waters.

Since then, Oolana's ghost has lured twenty young male
swimmers and one girl to their deaths. Even up to the
present, hikers and swimmers ignore the warning signs
and are pushed and pulled by some invisible force. Many
have seen Oolana's ghostly face and outstretched arms
seeking revenge for her precious lover. Babinda Boulders
is surrounded by glorious rainforest where locals and
tourists swarm into the dangerous rock pools to swim in
this heavenly area with its mountainous trees and huge
butterflies. The pools are enticing in such hot steamy
weather, but being so deep and with many large boulders
and crevasses many are at risk of drowning, due to
Babinda being one of the wettest towns in Australia and
prone to flash flooding. The water can become rough like
a washing machine, and the white churning water has no
buoyancy. It's a super terrifying phenomenon. Our family
used to live nearby, but then it didn't have many warning
signs and their four kids and friends had amazing days
enjoying the swimming and the BBQ's in this glorious
rainforest full of platypus, turtles, spiders, snakes and
cassowaries. Beware of the cassowary too.

THE MENCE OF HANGING CLOUDS
Robyn Lee

It was 2011 the year of some of the most devastating floods we had experienced in the state and without realising it at the time, the cloud phenomenon I saw on this particular day was a sign of things to come. It was the usual overcast muggy summer day and I had to make a trip to the supermarket, a chore that I had put off for long enough. I needed to buy the necessities for myself as well as some food for my two spoilt cats. God help me if I forgot that! Sighing, I looked up at the clouds and hoped I'd make it to the shopping centre and back before the forecast rain began. By the time I came out of the supermarket, the day had become significantly darker. I glanced up at the lowering clouds and stopped dead in my tracks. I had never seen clouds of that shape before. Filled with the rain that promised to spill, the clouds hung over me like half spheres, threatening to drop their load at any moment. I could only stop and stare, mesmerised by what I was seeing. "Bloody hell!" I heard a male voice beside me. It was a neighbour and he too was gazing awestruck at the sight. "We'd better get home before that lot hits us." We both ran to our respective cars and to my relief, I reached home and managed to get my shopping inside just as the first heavy drops started to fall. I had taken a couple of shots of the menacing phenomenon with my phone and on arriving home fired up my trusty computer and began searching for information. I didn't know the meteorological name for the clouds and after trying various phrases on Mr Google it came up with a photograph of identical clouds. They were called *mammatus* clouds because of their breast-like shape, caused by cold air dropping down and swelling the clouds resulting in rain or snow. In this case, it was the start of a severe weather event right through the region, resulting in dangerous flash flooding and homes destroyed.

NATURE'S MIRACLE
June Dowling

Sun filtered through the leaves,
Glistened the leaves covered with early morning drizzle.
Incessant barking filled the morning air,
Sounding first a warning, then distress.
Something was wrong.

I rounded the corner of the house
There stood my dog as if cemented to the path.
Ears upright, tail straightened and hairs standing
upright along her back.
Clear warning of imminent danger.

Before her were two seven foot long pythons.
The sun reflected on their fluorescent shiny skins.
Having shed their old skins for spring.

They danced and entwined each other,
Rising upwards to half their height like an
Indian charmers serpent.
They mouthed one another as they continued their
dancing ritual.

As quickly as their dance had begun
they separated, flattened their bodies to the ground,
slithered between the rocks and wire fence
heading for the bush ahead.

How lucky were we to witness this mating ritual.
The universe had shown us its magic and
announced the arrival of spring.

UNIDENTIFIED

FLYING

OBJECTS

RECHARGE
Elizabeth Lippiatt

"Position now correct for the recharge, captain," stated the pilot as she stabilized the motion of the spaceship. She continued with, "I'm surprised at the strength of the energy we're receiving. This recharge should not take long."

"Yes, that's why it was chosen. This large rock is over the intersection of two powerful Ley Line energy channels of this planet. Also, this area is sparsely populated."

"Sparsely populated? There is movement down there." After a while the pilot continued, "It's an amazingly huge rock all by itself in the middle of a flat desert plain. It's a pity the Galactic Federation does not allow us here; I would really like to explore it." She paused and then sharply said, "The security vessels from the Galactic Federation have moved in closer to us."

"Be extra alert," demanded the captain. "The passengers we have on board are dangerous and will try to escape."

"They wanted our energy drained. They delayed and delayed our departure until we really had to fight to pull away from the black hole that their planet was being pulled into."

"Yes, resulting in the necessity for us to recharge here. Exactly what they were after, the chance of escaping to this very planet."

"What would happen if they did?"

"The inhabitants would be at their mercy. There are important reasons why these ones are locked away and must continue to be."

"I understand their new home world is appropriately prepared just for them?"

"Yes, and it has been for a while. So be very alert. Any sign of a problem and we must act instantly."

An alarm started sounding.

"Captain, there is a problem with the passengers!" the pilot's voice competed with the alarm.

"Further lock down measures being activated," declared the
captain as he quickly manipulated his controls. "I was hoping those measures would not be necessary as they are brutal and the security vessels with us are so obvious."

"The security vessels have come in even closer," stated the pilot.

"Yes, they are ready to attach energy tethers onto us if necessary, so that we are held in place during the recharge. Those tethers would only be released when we leave for the passengers' new planet."

Horrified the pilot gasped, "Something is trying to take control from me!"

"Employing the emergency override control measures," the captain's controls now flashed red as he manipulated them and the spaceship heaved and rocked before settling down. The controls and propulsion system of the spaceship were now inactive, and it was being held in place for the recharge by energy tethers to the security vessels that totally surrounded it.

Moments passed as everyone eagerly waited for the pilot's declaration of,

"We are recharged!" Exactly the instant that statement was made the spaceship was towed by the security vessels rapidly out into the stratosphere of the planet. From there, still closely under guard, it would continue its journey to deliver its passengers to their new home world.

FEARING THE UNKNOWN
Lindy Standage

The Five Trans Australian Airlines (T.A.A.) engineers sat mesmerized during a smoko break. They were sitting near the runaway watching the brilliant flashing lights coming from weird shaped flying objects that were whirling low down in the sky.

The men were puzzled and felt worried. Harry the leading hand drew deeply on his cigarette and pointed upwards, "What on earth is that?"

Kevin went pale, "I've heard about Aliens taking humans back to their planet for tests."

"Oh hell!" exclaimed Jack. "No way. But they could cause a collision!"

"Back to work boys. Lots to do this arvo!"

The Melbourne Age, The Herald and The Sun newspapers the next day were full of the sightings, making people very nervous.

"Maybe they are friendly?" Jack said the next day.

"No!" answered Kevin. "Our planes could crash into them."

"Do you remember that young pilot that disappeared over the Bass Strait near Tasmania? He radioed to the Tower to say a strange object was above him with many lights glaring. Then after reporting this he completely vanished and his plane never found. His family never got over it; gives everyone the shivers!"

There have been so many sightings over Australia, terrifying and puzzling many. At Westall High School in Melbourne at 11 a.m. on Wednesday 6th April 1966, two hundred students and their teachers watched a silvery cigar shaped object fly over the school and land behind some trees in a paddock nearby. It was the size of a family car and flew off twenty minutes later at high speed. Military officials threatened a teacher, and anyone else who sighted the cigar shaped object, with dire consequences if they ever reported their stories to the newspapers. Maybe the truth will come out one day.

AN ALIEN CROSS
Nerida Marshall

Isolation and the dark can cause a simple thing like an unfamiliar noise or light to be given supernatural explanations. So, you may believe what I am about to share with you as a fanciful, imaginative story or an accurate description of what unfolded before me in the deserted wilds of outback Australia late one night. I still had 600 kilometres to get home on a trip fraught with flat tyres, giant roos, road kills and a punctured fuel tank. I was hot, hungry, smelly and totally fed up with my chosen career as an investigative journalist. Like most isolated travellers at that hour I just wanted to see the light of home but a six hour drive was still ahead. My air con had conked out and my radio had no reception. To top it all off my German Shepherd guard dog was farting out her dinner of a cold chicken pie, I swear, just to get back at me for not letting her swim in a croc infested river before we left the last town just on dark. In front of me the highway had leveled off to pancake flat and straight as a gun barrel. In the distance was a dim white glow. No matter how fast I drove it seemed to remain just on the horizon. An hour went by with no other traffic and unusually no horses, cattle, or even kangaroos on the road. I must have been getting closer because the ball of light was growing larger and brighter.

Ever so slowly the top of the sphere began to elongate towards the sky. I wondered to myself if it was a tracker beam going back to an alien UFO. Every sci-fi movie I had ever watched began flashing through my mind. But there was nowhere to hide. This area was treeless, mountain-less and farmhouse-less so I just kept going. Another hour had passed and the ball of light had now extended beams out sideways. With each kilometre closer it was forming more and more into a cross.

Was it simply waiting for me, a lonely traveler, to make my car stop and use its tracker beams to take me up into the mother ship? Was I over tired and hallucinating? Or maybe even asleep and my wrecked car and broken body would be found in the morning by some long-distance trucker unable to help because my farting dog would not let him near me.

Would the police eventually come, shoot my dog and airlift me to the hospital where I would be declared dead and my mum would cry and dad would say it was no place for a girl out there.

"Snap out of it before you kill us both." I actually yelled out loud almost frightening my dog into a heart attacked.

I was approaching the base of the cross when a massive semi-trailer with all lights blazing flew over a small rise blinding me in its white lights. It roared passed violently shaking the car. I had hit the brakes and stopped dead in my lane. Gradually my sight returned and the alien cross was now gone. Did the monstrous truck destroy the alien's intension to kidnap me? I will let you decide.

UFOs? WHAT UFOs?
Robert Young

Lights were starting to glow on the horizon as we headed west from the Gold Coast towards Alice Springs, or 'The Alice' as it is known. Having heard tales of UFO sightings in and around this town we decided to see for ourselves, so we hitched the caravan to the back of the fourby, loaded enough supplies for a month and headed off. The excitement rose a notch when we saw the glow low in the western sky.

Pulling into a rest stop for the night I turned to Sharon, my constant companion of some thirty years and said, "Tomorrow we will be there, in the capitol of UFO sightings in good old Aus."

"Not quite," came the cheeky reply. "The centre is supposed to be in Wycliffe Wells, just a little bit north of The Alice."

Smiling I retorted, "A mere 380 kilometres, a drop in the bucket in a country as big as this."

We sat and looked at the clear night sky, alive with stars from horizon to horizon as we enjoyed our light meal.

"I could just sit and look at this all night," I said very quietly as if not wanting to disturb the all encompassing silence. All I got in reply was an equally quiet grunt of agreement.

We were woken at dawn by what seemed like a swarm of a million budgerigars, calling as they wheeled enemas all around us as they came into the creek we had parked beside. They kept us company as we had breakfast, then broke camp and headed off to search for the elusive UFO's. We were surprised to see so many more like-minded people there when we arrived late that afternoon. As we set up camp, people wandered over and started to talk everything they knew about local sightings and informed us that we had come just at the right time as this was when the sightings were mostly seen.

Leaving just on dusk, we all drove a few kilometres away from the town lights, then settled down to wait and see what, if anything, we would see. As the time dragged on towards midnight, a few of the skeptics called it a night and headed back to the campsite. About one thirty in the morning, someone yelled, "There, there's one," as they pointed skywards.

Everybody looked towards the direction they were pointing as the chatter grew.

"No," someone offered, "That's just a satellite."

Suddenly there was a bright light dropping fast towards us and we all froze. Someone screamed as the light exploded in a huge flash then petered out as it burned up.

"Damn! Just a piece of space junk," someone said as we all settled back down and waited and waited.

A week later, we were amongst the last to leave and head home, wondering if the sightings we had been told about were real, or if it was just a ploy to draw tourists into one of the most beautiful parts of Australia.

VISITORS IN THE NIGHT
June Dowling

Her eyes stared upwards transfixed on the geometric pattern that swirled on the ceiling. Tiny red lights flashed intermittently. She had seen this before, in a dream maybe? Eyes closed she touched the sheets for reassurance, but sleep eluded her, lights and patterns filled her mind. Daybreak, coffee in hand she stumbled outside and settled on the old sofa. Her attention was drawn to the impression of a circle imprinted on the dewy grass. She noticed the surrounding hedge had also been flattened.

"Well I never," she cried. "I must have had visitors."

No, there was no logical explanation, she puzzled. What was this? She decided not to mention it to anybody. She knew her friends already thought her strange due to her spiritual beliefs. She knew the universe was full of possibilities if she was open to them.

The following night she eventually succumbed to sleep, even though she was full of anticipation and curiosity. A soft beep stirred her. She opened her eyes, the familiar geometric pattern danced across her ceiling and brilliant light illuminated her room.

She stared in awe then closed her eyes in disbelief. When she opened them again she was confronted by two silvery, elongated figures with dome shaped heads.

There were two black holes where there should have been eyes. It was as if she was glued to her bed. Nothing moved. She no longer had control of her body.

Not a word was spoken but in her thoughts resounded their every word. "This one's too lively. Be quick. Get it done."

Heat seared her chest and she fought to breathe. Then she felt as if a dozen needles pricked her stomach. Pain racked her body. She blinked and when she fully opened her eyes the silvery figures had vanished. All the lights went out and she was left once more in darkness. She hovered the rest of the night between wakefulness and sleep.

When she awakened with the morning sun she was delighted to be in her own bed.

"What a nightmare," she murmured as she prepared to shower. As warm water trickled down her chest pain gripped her. She looked downward and found a decent sized burn mark on her left breast and small pinhead sized holes in her stomach.

"What the ..." she cried. Her thoughts turned to the previous night. She grabbed her towel, wrapped it around herself and raced outdoors. There was a second indented circle on her lawn and the hedge had been flattened more than before. Now she would tell her friends, she decided. She shouted, "Now they'll have to believe me! I knew that night visitors from space were a possibility."

DREAMTIME

SPIRITS

SHIMMERING SANDS
Nerida Marshall

When Europeans first saw a platypus they immediately thought it to be a hoax: a creature hobbled together, Frankenstein style, from bits and pieces of known animals. Of course, this was not true but the legend behind the platypus creation is far darker than a mere hoax. It involves two young aboriginal boys who wanted to fish in a billabong with a silver shimmering bottom, but their eldest brother would not allow it. "But why? They demanded. "The water is so clear you can see the silver sand at the bottom and it is filled with big fat fish." Their brother explained patiently, "Because when I was a child my elders would not allow me to fish there. There is a very ancient and dangerous spirit in its waters. I obeyed my elders and so must you!" As the boys walked away disgruntled, they began to mock their brother's explanation, "He is jealous because we are braver than him. Or maybe he was being punished for something and doesn't want us to know. He walks around like a mighty warrior in the daytime but probably stays in his hut at night shivering like a frightened child."

They laughed at this absurd image as their older brother was very brave and a great hunter. He would one day even be the leader of their clan. Then, as if both boys had the same thought at the same time they smiled at each other mischievously and rushed off to get their fishing spears. They snuck past the huts towards the forest and, when no one was looking, they headed towards the forbidden billabong. Its sands were shimmering in the sunlight just like the fat fish in its waters. As hunters they should have taken notice of the lack of bush noises. Not a bird called, not an insect scurried. They raised their spears ready to strike but these dropped from their webbed claws and could no longer hold a spear. They now swim above the shimmering sands as platypuses with all the others who had disobeyed the warning of their elders. If you are ever warned to keep away from a certain billabong I really urge you to obey.

THE WAY HOME
Elizabeth Lippiatt

After a very successful hunt all the jubilant hunters were celebrating as they carried their bounty back to the tribe's camp site. They were unaware in their excitement that they had left one of their number behind. Koa had deposited himself under a tree unwilling to exert himself further. He felt the hunters of the tribe were obviously happy without him. Whether he was tired from or with the hunting he was not sure and partially hidden had promptly fallen asleep.

Koa awoke later to tinkling giggles. He looked around but could see no-one. Then he became aware that the shadows on the nearby the rocks were moving. At his gasp of alarm the giggles started again.

"Who are you?" Koa demanded and the giggling continued.

"We are the Mimi and you are now here with us."

"No! I! Where is everyone?" horrified Koa looked around to discover that he was alone and at the mercy of Mimi spirits.

"You know your way back to your tribe don't you?" asked the Mimi with teasing in their voice.

Koa could now see the thin human forms of the spirits as they danced around him. His panic continued as he wildly looked around trying to work out the way he needed to go to escape.

"As a trained and practised hunter you should easily be able to find the hunters' tracks and follow them back to your camp site," the Mimi continued.

"I, I'm not a good tracker," Koa ashamed admitted. At this the Mimi spirits all stilled.

"Why is that?" the Mimi asked.

"I was not good at it. I, I maybe didn't concentrate hard enough!" Koa sobbed.

"And now what are you going to do?"

"Now it's too late. If they don't come back for me I'm going to die!" Koa now truly wailed regretting all his prior inattention to his training.

"Calm. We will show you how to track your way home. But first we will fully enjoy ourselves with you."

Mimi games of fun and mischief now became fully under way. Koa joined in and had a wonderful time playing with the Mimi. He enjoyed their magical kingdom in and among the rocks and shadows until he felt that his tribe was grieving. His tribe had looked for him and having not found him, were now grieving as they believed he was no longer alive. Koa could not allow this. He wanted to go home.

As Koa was now spoiling their happy games the Mimi agreed again to help him to track his way back to his tribe's camp site. As the sprightly Mimi danced around him the shadows moved. They moved in such a way that the outline of the individual footprints became clearer. They showed the indented part of the footprint darker in the increased shadow. Surprised, Koa found he could now see the tracks and these were the homeward bound tracks of his tribe's hunters. Koa now happily tracked his way home.

JOSH MCEWAN AND THE MIMI
Bev Stewart

It was the final year of Josh's primary school education with School of the Air. Josh had enjoyed his telephone relationships with his teacher and friends, even though he had never met them face to face. Most of his mates were the sons and daughters of other remote station owners like his dad. Overhearing his parents arguing about his future education filled Josh with trepidation as his dad was insisting Josh be sent to TSS boarding school in Southern Queensland far from his home in Kakadu. Josh spoke about this to his local mate, Jimmy, the son of a leader of the aboriginal mob the Gagadu-speaking people who came from the north of the Arnhem Land escarpment area.

"Too far for walk-about!" Jimmy shook his head. They decided on a walk-about up north to Arnhem Land, where Jimmy's golli (grandma) lived. Jimmy led the way and at night they slept in the cool under billions of stars after a tasty bbq of Kangaroo tail.

Police had been alerted of the 'lost boy' as were multiple aeroplanes and helicopters. Many horsemen and aboriginal trackers were also called in.

"Not lost! He not wanna be found," said the aboriginal trackers each time the McEwan's cried about their lost boy. But they took no notice of the trackers. Eventually they concluded that Josh was lost in the remote bush country north of the station. After many hot days of walking, Josh and Jimmy stopped to shade from the blasting sunlight in the escarpment area in Arnhem Land. Jimmy navigated the way back to his grandma's home by his navigative singing. She was delighted to see her grandson and his friend and welcomed them with the smoke ceremony. That night again under billions of stars, they dined on goanna and Jimmy's golli droned on telling the Dreamtime stories. While the golli's stories were recited, the bbq fire began to die down. Josh became aware of the stillness and listened to the silence which inherited the night. Watching the billions of barely moving stars, Josh began to lose wakefulness. Stillness, silence, sleepers seemed to release an eeriness into the world. The eeriness of sound, as low as could barely be heard began to emanate from the escarpment's caves. Invisible movement began to emerge from the rocky caves accompanied by the eerie wailing sounds like Theremin electrophones. Just wailings; no tunes, no singing, only weird continuous sounds releasing occasional giggles. Josh was confused. Was he dreaming? Were these the Mimi spirits the golli had told him about? Rather than being aggressive they seemed to be laughing, giggling, floating spirits having fun! They flicked his nose and set his hair on end. Jimmy and his golli were still soundly asleep and the Mimi seemed to avoid them, but they encircled Josh with swooping waves of nose clips and electrophonic swoops as Josh walked away. Happily taking stock of his situation and the Mimi visits to his semi-consciousness Josh realised he could never leave this precious area of his world in the Northern Territory. He belonged here just like his mate Jimmy.

GHOST

SHIPS

HERE BE DRAGONS
Nerida Marshall

She emerged from the salty mists silent as a ghost. Her bare ribs exposed to the elements of eons. Stripped of all her glory; just a shell of her former self but still defiant to the winds and seas. Her ghostly crew is now scattered bones within the ocean depths. Her bowsprit defiantly points upwards towards the stars.

These same stars had coursed across the heavens ignorant to the trepidation of a sea captain and crew as they entered uncharted waters three hundred years ago. Jagged fingers of coral reef had ripped apart their ship plank by plank as the roaring ocean slammed into her sides and forced its way deep into her hull.

As defenseless and broken as her crew she spiraled down tearing herself apart on the rocks and reefs until at last she lay still on the sandy bottom. So deep was she that the raging currents pulled by the wax and wane of the moon could not touch her. Eventually her fate drifted into the pages of legend and myth. A glorious ship ladened with treasures and lost near a mysterious unknown continent where only 'here be dragons' was written on the maps of her time and for centuries to follow.

But now she is open to the sun and seagulls after a mighty storm dislodged her from her sandy grave and hoist her up on the turbulent waves to be dumped violently onto this whitest of white beach. Powdery sands now trickled through her broken boards and missing deck replacing the spaces once filled by water.

How long will she remain here in this desolate place being no more than home for crabs and a look out post for hungry Sea Eagles? Her ancient, waterlogged timbers will soon dry out in the blistering sun making them like brittle bones. The unrelenting climate of this new continent will make short work of her remains.

If she is not found soon she, her treasure, and the fate of her crew will remain forever gliding between the reality of her existence and rejection of the modern world that she ever existed at all. Such is the fate of those brave souls who have drifted, by desire or fate, too close to the land of 'here be dragons'.

A GHOSTLY ACT
Elizabeth Lippiatt

"Derrick, I don't like that we are here in this weather," declared Belinda as she handed him a drink and sat down to enjoy her own.

"Why, my love? You usually enjoy the fact that we are cut off in this weather."

"You may be fine but this time I have to go out again this afternoon for that medical appointment," she shrugged.

"Look at it!" Belinda gestured at the window. "Fog so thick we cannot see anything at all outside the windows. And I have never heard the waves pounding so heavily on the rocks. How I long for a wind to blow that fog away." She paused, "It's easy in these conditions to see how an early sea going vessel without present day navigation equipment could have got themselves into trouble." Belinda felt sure she had started babbling inanely, as something was really worrying her.

"We have always loved it here in strong weather; our privacy being practically assured. I will not give up my alone time with you and the boys."

Derrick now looked at her with a query in his eyes.

"What is the problem?" He asked slowly as Belinda had got up and was walking around in an agitated manner. They could hear a vibrant noise from the rumpus room.

"Hear that? All that noise comes from when we took them around the Great Ocean Road and showed them where the shipwrecks were, especially the Loch Ard. And then you are just too good at your profession!" She declared loudly.

"Acting?" Derrick laughed. "Why what's up now?" he demanded.

"You acted it out to us; all that happened on those ships. It all became real to the boys and now they are in their playroom acting out all the roles and circumstances you portrayed. And of course, little Timmy has added his favourite pirates to the mix."

47

"Well then," Derrick said carefully. "It all sounds like they are having fun and this weather completes the picture." Suddenly she added with desperation in her voice, "I keep feeling something is wrong. I'm all on edge."

Very quickly his reassuring smile turned to alarm as their boys came rushing at them in great distress. They were wildly gesturing at the window. When Derrick and Belinda looked at the window, they became aware that the fog was gone and what could be seen clearly was a sailing ship being driven by enormous waves onto the rocks. A mast was down, and shredded sails were flapping from the other two. Disbelieving what they were all seeing Belinda kept saying, "It's a sailing ship! It's a sailing ship! This can't be real."

Horrified they watched as the huge waves drove the ship steadily closer and closer to the rocks. Before they could get over the shock and think of anything they could do about it, the ship simply disappeared.

SINK OR SAIL
Robert Young

Built in Tasmania in the mid 1950's, the ship Patanela, a seventy-five-foot twin masted schooner, had a steel hull and engine which made it unusual for the time. Used for ferrying scientists to Antarctica then as a cray fishing boat, before being bought by a Western Australian businessman who intended to use it as a tourist boat in the waters of north Queensland.

After a full refit in Fremantle, the ship set sail with the owner sailing as far as Esperence, with the skipper's daughter disembarking in Port Lincoln in South Australia. This left Ken Jones, a very experienced deep-water skipper, aboard with his wife and two young deckhands, John Blissett and Michael Calvin.

When the boat sailed into Portland Victoria, the skipper rang the owner and asked for $500 for petrol but did not purchase any, even though they had been motoring and not using the sails.

After restocking with some supplies, they set sail and were seen motoring past a lighthouse in Jervis Bay south of Sydney on November the 7th. In the early hours of the morning of November 8th, the Patanela arrived off the coast of Botany Bay. At two and a half minutes to one, the following message was received.

"Sydney Radio, Sydney radio, this is Patanela on channel 16, do you read"?

"Patanela, Sydney. Loud and clear. Over."

"Patanela, I believe we have run out of fuel. We're approximately ten miles east of Botany Bay. We've hoisted our sails and we're tracking out to the east, so tracking about 080."

A second message followed about an hour later causing much mystification for a later hearing into the events of the voyage.

"How far is Moruya? We're unfamiliar with that position. How far south is it in miles from us?"

A little later a third message, then static.

"300ks south…… is it south?" Static then silence and the Patanela was never heard from again.

No explanation was ever given for the disappearance of the Patanela, but a sighting of a ship answering to its description was reported by a retired police officer sometime later. He identified it by a photograph in a boating magazine, checking it out through binoculars when they were both at anchor, but when he asked for it to identify itself, they denied it was the Patanela despite its blue paint and square portholes, a very distinctive design indeed. The ship weighed anchor shortly afterwards and disappeared, never to be seen again.

MYTHICAL CREATURES

OUR MOUNT SURPRISE SURPRISE – A TRUE STORY
Nerida Marshall

I think I have read every story about every mysterious creature supposedly haunting Australia's mountains and bush land. Like most other people I would be enthralled but also disbelieving, treating them as no more than fairy stories or folklore. Until I had reason to doubt these logical dismissives and wonder at the possibility of what creatures are out there that we humans might rarely, if ever, encounter. It was 1973 and my fiancé and I had gone to the Mount Surprise gem fields to search for topaz. Our first night was spent camping next to a crystal-clear billabong filled with fat silvery fish. Above us the most magnificent night sky was a rampant traffic jam of shooting stars, blinking satellites, and unknown whizzes of light from who-knows-what other sources.

In the kookaburra dawn we headed up the creek towards its headwaters. We stopped at each likely spot to try our luck at finding some smooth water-washed and unfractured gems, hopefully in a beautiful translucent blue that was much in demand. By midday we had reached the last waterfall which was flowing from a small tabletop plateau. It was completely bare red dirt with not a tree or bush or even a struggling piece of grass. In the centre was an odd pile of rocks forming a largish cave. In front of the cave's entrance were clumps of matted fur and bones scattered about like a warning. Not afraid to let it be known that you were in its territory. These were not large bones like cattle or horses but not small like those of rabbits but more the size of fully grown kangaroos. It was not a very high cave so we assumed it would not be big enough for seven-foot Yowie to habitat if such things existed.

Now it was broad daylight. A beautiful brilliant sunny Queensland day. The trees along the creek were in flower but there were no bird calls or even the usual droning of the cicadas. It was ominously still and deathly quiet. And then we smelt it. An indescribable smell of 1,000 horrors, straight out of nightmares. A smell so terrible that it coursed past the analytical part of our brains right into the primal fight or flight section and that is exactly what we did. We fled down the rocks alongside that waterfall like we could fly. Sheer terror kept our footing sure all the way to our camp and I can tell you there was no stargazing that night. We locked the doors to our camper and spent the night listening for whatever lived in that cave to come and try to drag us back to its lair. Once the sun rose enough to see the track out we were gone. I've always wanted to go back armed with a shotgun, just in case, and tie some cameras to the trees to see just what mysterious creatures actually lived there.

WELL, IMAGINE THAT
Robert Young

Ya know, I used to work on a cattle property in western Queensland. I was a general dog's body. Whatever needed doing, I did it. At one stage, we had busloads of Japanese tourists coming in. Some stayed just for the day, and some stayed for a week to experience life on the land. When the day trippers came, I was always prepared, if a little, all right, a bloody lot mystified by the fact that these wallies would bring these brand-new pairs of jeans that they had paid hundreds of dollars for, and pay me to shoot holes in the bloody things. Crazy beggars! Anyways, one evening we were sitting around a campfire with those staying the week enjoying the bar-be-que, when there was a great crash from just outside the light from the fire. Everybody, except me of course, started getting excited as Reg came running into the light looking like an axe murderer was hot on his heels. "Bloody thing, it nearly got me that time," he cried as he grabbed a burning piece of wood and raced off into the darkness, yelling and screaming like a banshee as he went. "What is out there?" came the frightened enquiry from the mob whose eyes opened so wide they looked European. "Oh," I said waving my hand in a dismissive manner, "it's just that pesky Drop Bear that tries to grab people who wander around at night unaccompanied." I had them well and truly hooked, and managing to keep a straight face, only just, I continued, "They live in tall trees and when you least expect it, they drop on you!" Using one of the boys, I mimicked an imaginary animal dropping with claws extended and grabbing on. A couple of the girls screamed as I latched onto young Tony, so I thought I would give them a couple of minutes to chatter excitedly amongst themselves before continuing with the story about the huge Bunyip that lived in the deep gorge at the side of the paddock, and advised them to never venture off without one of the hands who would be fully armed to protect them, should Billy the wild Bunyip ever make his presence known. Silly bloody tourists!

PICNIC TIME
Elizabeth Lippiatt

"What a beautiful day and such a lovely place. How did you find it Penny?" asked Lily as they walked alongside a bubbling water course. They swung a picnic basket between them.

"Ben told me of it when I said I didn't want us to stay all day at the winery with them."

Surprised Lily said, "I thought he seemed angry when we left."

"Yes. But he knows I just can't stay playing the dutiful female appendage all the time." Penny grimaced as she said this.

"We did have a wonderful time last night listening to the stories of his ancestors. You both seemed happy then," Lily exclaimed.

"It's one sided! I have to agree with him and listen to him all the time!"

"Could it be he has an inferiority complex and he's trying to prove himself?"

"Yes. But he's not getting any better. I can't always keep praising him!" Penny's voice sounded strangled with frustration. After that they both continued to walk in silent contemplation.

"Oh this is nice!" stated Lily. They had come to where a lake was separated from the watercourse. Reflected in the still water of the lake were the varying greens of the overhanging trees, reeds and ferns.

"Yes. Ben said there was a lovely Billabong here. He knows the type of places where I like to be. He said we would be private here as there were stories about it containing a Bunyip."

"A Bunyip? What's that?" Lily's eyebrows were raised in query.

"Oh you, English person," laughed Penny.

"Yes, I know. I'm in Australia now so you can call me an ill-educated pom," Lily grinned in reply.

"Well, it's a mythical aboriginal creature that lives in Billabongs, lakes and swamps and so on."

"Ah!" said Lily. "But does it eat people?"

"According to the stories, can do," stated Penny. She tried to be dead faced but couldn't hold it.

"Oh well," Lily said, continuing to smile. "This is a lovely spot let's have our picnic quickly before the Bunyip arrives and wants to join in by eating us."

They both laughed at this, spread the blanket and enjoyed their picnic. After they had eaten and packed away the food Penny asked, "I hope you have been truly enjoying your stay with us?"

"Oh yes. Of course there are the usual little things. You know the flies and I am trying to get used to the noise of the Cicadas."

"Yes, they can get deafening."

As they listened the noise of the Cicadas stopped. There was complete silence.

In a hushed voice Lily asked, "Um, Penny, why is it silent?

Penny stood up, "Let's go! Run!" she yelled grabbing Lily's hand as she started to run.

A rushing sound was heard behind them, and they both turned toward the Billabong to see a large dark green creature rising up in the middle of the water. Both screamed and ran as fast as they could.

BUNYIP'S SPACE
Elizabeth Lippiatt

They are in my space.
This space is meant for me.
I live here in grace.
I live here to be free.

The two walk here.
Noisy, chattering, annoying me.
In a while I'll make it clear,
here they must not be.

I watch. I wait.
Away they have not gone.
I pause and delay.
Now they have not long.

They are in my space.
This space is meant for me.
I live here in grace.
I live here to be free.

I stir, I rise.
The air goes still.
A Bunyip they cry,
and run shrieking shrill.

They were in my space.
A space meant for me,
To live here in grace,
To live here to be free.

HEED THE WARNING
June Dowling

"Tell us a story of when you were a boy grandpa," chorused my grandchildren, as I tucked them into bed.

"Something scary in the bush," added Simon the youngest one.

"I have one from long ago when I was ten. Your age Jack," I replied. This memory was as vivid as it was 60 years ago. It all began one very hot humid day, just like today."

"In the bush pa?" Jack asked.

I continued, "I was sick of sitting on the veranda swatting flies and asked my grandmother if I could visit my Aboriginal friend Jimmy from down the road and go fishing in the river."

"You liked holidays in the bush with your grandma," Jack interjected.

I continued, 'Now ye mind,' grandma said. 'Don't ye be going down to the billabong, the Bunyip i'll get ye and I'll never see ye again. Be back by supper or pa I'll give ye a whipping.'

I feared the billabong. I had heard the old timers' stories of children who went there and never came back.

I answered ma, 'No it's the river for us. We'll get you fish for supper,' Ma chuckled. 'That'll never happen.'

It was common knowledge that we caught no fish but loved our dip in the river. I met Jimmy, he was at the end of the driveway, 'We going fishing?' he asked. 'Sure thing,' I replied. 'Let's go to the billabong. I heard it sparkles with gold,' he said.

I replied, 'I promised ma we wouldn't and you know the stories of kids disappearing there.'

'Yes, the Elders speak of evil spirits but I reckon that's to stop us finding the gold,' Jimmy replied.

"Gold's precious!" exclaimed Simon.

"Yes," I replied. "We wanted to see that gold. So we trekked a long way in the heat. When we arrived Jimmy stripped off and jumped in. I screamed at him to get out but he didn't hear me. He was so certain that there was gold and dived

58

under water once more. He never came up. I yelled and yelled. I could see a gold sparkle but no Jimmy."

"Jimmy died?" stammered Jack and Simon began to cry. Just at that moment my daughter popped her head around the bedroom door. "You frightening the kids again dad. I'll never get them to sleep tonight."

"No. I just made up a story so they would pay attention to their Elders."

"You made the story up pa? Jimmy didn't die?" asked Jack. Simon sighed, wiped his eyes and said, "You didn't go to the billabong?"

"Yes, but Jimmy was rescued and we were friends for years and years."

Luckily, they asked no more questions and cuddled down to sleep. My memories flooded my mind and I shed a tear as I left their room. I knew the truth about how bad the evil spirits could be.

AUSTRALIAN

BUSH POEMS

THE SWAGGIE'S PICTURE SHOW
Robert Young

The dust stirs as his feet fall in a steady rhythm
as he heads for his next destination.
His swag rests lightly upon his back,
his billy swinging freely to and fro.

Reaching a favourite spot beside the creek,
he fills his billy and sets it in the fire,
then he settles down to watch it boil
as he enjoys the sounds of the bush around him.

As he waits for his billy to boil
he hears the warble of the magpie,
he hears the caw of the crow,
for him, these are the music of life.

They keep him happy and alive
for they are his picture show.
This is the life of a swaggie
as he wanders to and fro.

BUSH LIFE CYCLE
June Dowling

A new day had begun
I walked around the garden
My heart and body was warmed by the summer sun.
Delight! I glanced towards a bush turkey nest.
Leaves were lifting in the air.
With anticipation, excitement, I settled down to wait.

A piece of egg surfaced.
Then a chick's head aloft in the air.
Miraculous! She was out!
She strutted among the leaf litter,
exploring the ground as she went.,
Pecking and looking for sustenance.
She breathed in the morning air unaware
of the threats that surrounded her.

She had begun her new life journey alone.
Reluctantly I left her to explore, as I ventured into my day.
Later that night I walked the driveway
and circled the garden looking for her.
Alas, she lay still upon the grass.
Her new life just begun had ended!
Sadness, then anger surfaced in me.
What creature had taken her life?
I would never know.

Fortunate I was, to have witnessed her birth
and kept her company for a short while.
Until mother nature made the call for her to go.
Bush life is hard, transitory, constantly changing.
Next morning the father bush turkey was back at work.
He heaped the leaves on his mound.
In eager preparation for the female to entice.
The bush life cycle has begun again.
While I wait, in anticipation for the next miracle.

BUSH COLOURS
Nerida Marshall

Bush colours are the colours of life and death.

Red dust devils dance before a storm as it blows the breath

of living into an arid land forcing forth a burst of life

in greens, dark to light, and flowers orange to yellow rife

with insects hatching or dying. Birds panting and scratching,

while the cunning wombat sleeps in his warren waiting

for the dewy coolness of the blue desert evening.

OUTBACK
GHOST TOWNS

REAL TALES OR NOT?

Robert Young

BANG! I sat bolt upright in bed. What was that I thought was it part of a dream or was there someone else here. After seven weeks living in a campervan by myself, I was ready for a bed that did not rock every time a road train went tearing past at 100 kilometres per hour. Parking outside the building near a sign that said BED AND BREAKFAST, I walked inside. The temperature was forty-three degrees Celsius outside, inside it was a comfortable thirty-five. The building was like the rest of the town, completely deserted. This was one of the many ghost towns in outback Australia; the mining had come and gone and the prospectors and workers with it. I walked through the whole building and found twenty beds that were dusty, but serviceable. Collecting my swag from the van I chose a very comfortable one. After flipping the mattress over, I bolted from the room to let the dust settle. I made myself a meal and enjoyed it sitting on the verandah at the front of the building, listening to the songs of the birds as they said goodnight to each other. Finally, I rose and walked into my room and was soon fast asleep.

BANG! I sat bolt upright in bed and reached for the powerful flashlight I had bought in with me. My heart thumped so hard I thought it might jump out of my chest. I sat listening but nothing more happened. I waited for what seemed an age but was probably just a few minutes before deciding it was part of a dream. I had just lain back down when I heard light footsteps coming down the passage towards the room I was in. They hesitated outside the door and then shuffled on towards the rear of the building. My curiosity got the better of me and I jumped out of bed, turned on the flashlight and flung open the door. No one was there. I shone the light back and forth and was just about to go out the back when I realised the only footprints in the dust on the floor were mine. Shaking my head, I pinched myself to make sure I really was awake. I was. Ah well, it was a ghost town after all. Rising early, I had a fry up for breakfast and hit the road to see what lay ahead.

Stopping at a small town later that day, I dropped into the local art gallery. When I told the friendly people there about my experience, they smiled knowingly and said, "But there is no such place. We often get travellers in here telling us about a place where they spent the night, but we know that it does not exist."

I had a good laugh with them about it, but they insisted it did not exist, so when I left, I drove back to where the town was the night before, and to this day, I have never been able to find that ghost town.

SHADOW DANCERS OF MAYTOWN
Nerida Marshall

Did you know that in the Australian outback, on a moonless night, the darkness is a thick layer-on-layer of blackness. People think that black is a solid, solitary colour but they are wrong. The black of the Australian outback is shades of shadows. A darkness that, within those layers, a perceptive eye might just catch the subtle, stealthy movement of beings maliciously waiting. I have felt them watching me when I camped alone.

They won't come when the evening fire is alive and bright; temporally staving off the terror and torments hiding in the dark. They withdraw back when I throw a large hardwood log onto the campfire. But when the fire has died, I won't hear them surrounding me, for they have no footfall. Cocooned in my sleeping bag I shimmy over as close as I dare to the fiery embers. Only if I can fight off sleep can I avoid their inevitably attack. But watching the dying embers is mesmerising and my eyelids grow heavier by the second. The lullabies of the flat plains curlews and the prancing brolgas make me so sleepy. As I drift off into that linear plane between life and the mini death of sleep the shadow beings begin their terror.

Just to taunt me they start by making the red earth tremble as I wonder if I'm awake or in a nightmare. Even with eyes wide open it is hard to tell in the all-engulfing inky night. They are plucking at my sleeping bag and pinching my toes. I can taste the red soil in my mouth as their dervish spinning and dancing around the dull embers causes a haze of fine dust to rise and slowly settle over my face and hair.

Longer than our time has been recorded have they existed here, longer even than the ancient ones who left their paintings on the cave walls of their hunts for the giant wombats and the monstrous creatures found in the long dead inland sea. Do they resent the presence of physical beings such as myself and the generations of tribes who had camped here before me? Or do they just get enjoyment from scaring us; some entertainment in an otherwise flat and boring land perhaps?

But the instant those fingers of sunlight reach the horizon I will be packed and gone and will never again ignore the advice from the local clans when they warn me not to camp on the site of this old ghost town.

It is not abandoned solely because the minerals ran out, they say, but because as the miners left and the population decreased the shadows grew closer to the huts and makeshift tents making it so much easier for these beings to creep in the darkness and wait. They wait to pounce on an unsuspecting human ripping at their throats and tearing at their clothes until finally each and every one had fled for their lives leaving the shadows to dance.

A PERFECT CONVENIENCE
Elizabeth Lippiatt

"We should be back on the right road by now!" grumbled Linda.

"You had to go and wouldn't do it near the road because of the trucks passing. I don't know why you had us to go so far to find the necessary spot."

Dana was frustrated and frightened now as she wasn't sure how to get back to the road they had been on. "I would have just squat down by the vehicle and if a truck or something came along, I would have hidden by opening a door."

Later they hit an extra bumpy section of road.

"I don't like this," complained Linda.

"You wanted privacy, so I took us down this dirt road until you were satisfied," stated Dana sharply. "Try your phone again to see if we can get reception, mine's totally out of battery. It would help if we could get a map and direction."

"No, nothing," said Linda softly as she shook her phone in frustration. Then she continued with, "I thought you knew the way! You said you did!"

"I have never needed to go off the main road before."

"So, it's my fault we are lost!" Linda loudly protested.

"Oh, there's a change here," Dana interjected. "We are joining a bigger dirt road."

"Such an improvement," Linda said sourly.

"It is an improvement and should go somewhere!" snapped Dana.

"There's something up ahead. We are getting somewhere. I am relieved. It is starting to get late," Linda's panic was showing.

"Yes, but where are we?"

"Welcome to Kuridala that old sign says," said Linda.

"Oh my God!" choked out Dana.

"Why? We are at a town now and we will get food, petrol and there will be a place to sleep!" Linda had brightened.

"No, Kuridala is a ghost town!" stated Dana.

"A ghost town!" Linda shrieked.

Linda whimpered as they drove into the town's main street. "It was a copper mining town before and during the first world war," Dana informed Linda as she tried to get her back into a more functioning frame of mind.

"Is there no-one here at all?" Linda continued to whimper.

"Tourists do come here. There may be."

"May be," Linda whispered slowly, terrified. And then she exclaimed, "What's that?" as she pointed to the remnants of the towering smelting chimneys. "I thought that they were buildings, like apartments! They're not though, are they?"

At this point Dana was trying not to laugh at her companion, especially as she felt that she herself could easily become hysterical. They walked around the town noting the abandoned facilities including the railway lines and cemetery.

When Dana noticed a sign warning visitors to watch their step as there were numerous unmarked mine shafts they could easily fall into. Reading this Dana muttered sourly to herself, "Well if you had to go and had no convenient tree, down there would be a very private place to go and do it!"

HISTORIC GEM
June Dowling

It was that time of year again. Kate sipped latte in her favourite cafe. She had completed the shopping demanded by Helen; one checkered shirt, boots, Akubra and belt with large buckle. This July was not going to be a lame Christmas in July dinner. She prayed it was no bush, camping or wildlife adventure.

Helen burst on the scene, full country girl regalia, while a hesitant Sue followed. "Ready for the greatest days of your life," she announced. "Bet you can't wait! No surly faces! We're off on the great Australian outback adventure; The Quamby Rodeo!"

"Oh my God, my worst nightmare, dust, flies, cow stench and camping," Kate groaned.

"It's all that and much more!" Helen continued, "Quamby was once a bustling railway village, twenty hours to our north. The pub was established 1860 but closed ten years ago due to disrepair. In April it was refurbished by two Gold Coast couples and in July the town swells from three to four thousand for the famous rodeo."

Sue responded, "No! No suitable transport!"

Kate stammered, "And I don't like cruelty to animals and grown men bucked from cows!"

"Bulls," Helen corrected, "and masses of single guys."

"There is that," conceded Sue and Kate.

"Everything's sorted," stated Helen. "I have Dave's dual cabin ute and gear. Lots of fun. Even a last race for outsiders. Free poncho and sombrero while you ride a donkey! We meet next Thursday 5pm my place. With one stop we'll reach Quamby Pub for dinner Friday. All settled!"

The trip was uneventful apart from loud music, singing, laughter, potholes and mintie chewing. They arrived at 6pm under the 'Welcome to Quamby Rodeo 2023' banner and joined a sea of utes, swags, Akubras and golden buckles.

Exhausted from a night of beer, steak and dancing they bunked down at midnight in the back of the ute.

Suddenly they were awakened to thunderous music over the loudspeakers. "Good morning sunshine ..." and the smell of breakfast in the air. They dragged their disheveled selves to join the crowd. After hours of bucking bulls, clowns and cheers Kate headed for quiet behind the pub where she found a large sparkling pool. The winter sun hit her eyes. Suddenly she saw a woman spread eagled laid face down in the water. "Help!" Kate screamed and ran towards the crowd. She frantically grabbed at Helen and Sue. "Save her," she yelled and pulled them towards the pool. A crowd of onlookers followed. "She was there, there!" Sue pointed. Helen declared, "Must have been a reflection."

An old bushie stroked his beard, "Nay, lass that was Irma the Quamby ghost. Lucky are you. Not many see her."

Kate was not feeling lucky. She averted her eyes downward to the tiled message on the pool below, 'Quamby Pub in the Scrub'. Kate muttered, "No more scrub for me!"

GONDWANALAND-

WHEN DINOSAURS ROAMED

THEY WERE REAL ONCE
Nerida Marshall

"Michelle, come here, quickly, quickly."

Michelle dropped her shovel and ran over to her excited friend. "What is it Chloe? We have been on this fossil dig for a week now and this is the first time I have heard you excited."

Chloe and Michelle were exchange students from a French University on a dig in the very edge of the once great inland sea. Australia's birthing place of unique prehistoric creatures.

A bone here and a claw there was all that the surrounding dust had given up since they had arrived. But now looking into the bank of dried out creek bed Michelle saw the tip of a very large bone.

"I think we had better call Joe over before we touch anything," said Michelle cautiously.

"No!" shouted Chloe. "Not yet. He is the head of this dig and might lay claim to its discovery. No, if we dig around it some more to see what it is then everyone will know it is our discovery. *Oui*?"

Michelle considered for a moment then answered excitedly, "If it is something very special, we could even get a PhD at our university. Let us dig!"

They laboured for hours in the blistering sun reluctant to give up their prize to Dr Joseph Myles, the palaeontologist in charge of this dig. He was a red-faced, raw-boned Aussie who had grown up in this central Queensland sheep country with its wealth of dinosaur bones before heading off to the city to study, turning his childhood interest into a successful career.

Joe finally found them on the verge of exhaustion in the centre of their hand dug circle surrounded by a collection of unusual bones. "What have you girls found?" Obviously, it was not a question he expected them to answer as they had no idea.

"We were coming to get you," stammered Michelle.

"*Qui*," added Chloe. "We just wanted to clear the dirt away first."

"And we did not touch the bones only the dirt," Michelle was guiltily tripping over her words.

"Girls, girls settle down," Joe drawled in his slow outback accent. "I think you have made a truly great find. Let's look at it closely. It is obviously not a sea creature or even a dinosaur. It's a large marsupial." He then pointed to the four lethal hooked claws at the end of an extended arm bone.

"So this creature is a large cat of some type?" asked Chloe

"No, no." Joe chuckled. "This is way more exciting than any predatory cat." He pointed to the large skull. "Look at those massive canine teeth. Oh, yes indeed, a mythical tree climbing Australian marsupial, deadly and elusive. It has now been discovered by two French girls who have travelled halfway across the globe. You, *ma cheries*, have found a *Nimbadon* commonly known as the legendary Drop Bear. A Dreamtime creature of the indigenous peoples' mythology, yet here it is; proving that they were real once."

GONDWANA, LAND OF THE GIANTS
Robert Young

Gondwanaland was formed when an area encompassing Australia, South America, Africa, India, Madagascar, Antarctica, and New Zealand broke from Gondwana approximately 200 MYA. The breakup continued as the countries moved around finally finishing where they are today. During this period, temperatures in Australia varied from hot and wet to what they are currently as the land mass rotated as it travelled south, and Antarctica broke off and finally settled further south. Despite the cooler range of Australia's temperatures, there are sufficient similar rocks and plants on the other countries to prove they were all once part of the supercontinent known as Gondwanaland. Dinosaurs are thought to have roamed in Queensland from the late Triassic period to middle Jurassic period due to footprints, which have been found near Winton in the west of the state.

These Theropod footprints are known to be from the early to mid-Cretaceous period, including the theropod ichnospecies as well as Skartopus and Tyrannosauropus found at the Lark Quarry dinosaur stampede site also near Winton. Trackways, the preserved footprints of dinosaurs and other species, can help fill the gaps in the fossil record when body fossils are rare. The largest dinosaur to live in Australia is the Australotitian Cooperensis. It is believed to have been thirty metres long and six and a half metres high from the ground to the hip and lived ninety-eight to ninety-five million years ago. The remains of this one were found in the Cooper Creek area of southwest Queensland and is considered in the top ten largest in the world. The largest dinosaur known at this time is the Titanosaur Patagotitan Mayourm, which lived in the country known today as Patagonia in Argentina. There are many records of dinosaurs in different parts of Australia of all sizes. Some were carnivores with some living on plants and grasses. It is believed they were wiped out when a huge rock split the earth's crust open causing long periods of acid rain and equally long periods without sunlight.

TERRA AUSTRALIS
Robyn Lee

Gaia moved, setting off a sequence of events. Mountains spewed forth fire and lava. Oceans rose and fell, their waters sweeping across vast continents which shook under the onslaught, creating massive fissures and crevasses and breaking off enormous tracts of land. One hundred and fifty million years ago, one of these gigantic pieces of land drifted away from Pangaea, its parent continent. During the slow journey to the south-east, the fledgling continent continued to evolve and became known as Gondwanaland to the scientists of the future.

Gondwanaland sloughed off smaller pieces over the centuries which developed in their own unique ways. One of the larger chunks came to a gradual halt in the southern hemisphere. It had a distinct shape and was ringed with inhospitable mountains surrounding a vast inland sea. Around its perimeter, many and varied islands were randomly scattered, eventually having their own distinct flora and fauna.

Over the following millennia, huge wondrous creatures developed from microbes, becoming winged and taking to the air or walking on four legs, sometimes two. A nomadic people arrived and made the newborn continent their home. Comets from outer space slammed into the continent creating enormous craters which would, over millions of years, create precious stones and minerals waiting to be discovered by generations to come. From microscopic seeds grew gigantic trees, many unusual bushes, shrubs and colourful flowers which would one day become a goldmine for botanists and scientists, giving up their secrets for the development of medicines.

Explorers would name this island "terra australis", meaning southern land, before it became Australia. The inland sea would evaporate to become desert and salt pan, eventually yielding its secrets, in the form of fossils, to the future inhabitants. As humans evolved, stories of a fabulous land in the south caused northern explorers to search for this huge continent. From their discovery and settlement of the new land began one of the most shameful periods in the recent history of Australia. The nomadic people of the great southern land were enslaved or killed and pushed into arid areas of the country, and the newly inhabited continent was declared Terra Nullius, land of no people. England deported their convicts, including children, to the distant land as punishment for the most minor infringements as well as for more serious crimes. With these unfortunates came disease, against which the original inhabitants had no immunity, alcoholism, venereal diseases, and murderous rampages.

Eventually, this broken-off piece of Gondwanaland would become my home, as it has for immigrants from all countries of the globe. Australia today is a country of many cities and towns populated by over 26,000,000 people but sadly, the original nomadic inhabitants have become used to the white man's ways with only a few isolated communities in the Outback where ancient traditions are still practiced.

Hopefully, time will come full circle and both black and white can live beside each other in harmony, learning from the land without destroying it and respecting Gaia once again.

www.ingramcontent.com/pod-product-compliance
Lightning Source LLC
Chambersburg PA
CBHW072042170626
46811CB00008B/3135

The Strength of the Strong by Jack London

John Griffith "Jack" London was born John Griffith Chaney on January 12th, 1876 in San Francisco.

His father, William Chaney, was living with his mother Flora Wellman when she became pregnant. Chaney insisted she have an abortion. Flora's response was to turn a gun on herself. Although her wounds were not severe the trauma made her temporarily deranged.

In late 1876 his mother married John London and the young child was brought to live with them as they moved around the Bay area, eventually settling in Oakland where Jack completed grade school.

Jack also worked hard at several jobs, sometimes 12-18 hours a day, but his dream was university. He was lent money for that and after intense studying enrolled in the summer of 1896 at the University of California in Berkeley.

In 1897, at 21 , Jack searched out newspaper accounts of his mother's suicide attempt and the name of his biological father. He wrote to William Chaney, then living in Chicago. Chaney said he could not be London's father because he was impotent; and casually asserted that London's mother had relations with other men. Jack, devastated by the response, quit Berkeley and went to the Klondike. Though equally because of his continuing dire finances Jack might have taken that as the excuse he needed to leave.

In the Klondike Jack began to gather material for his writing but also accumulated many health problems, including scurvy, hip and leg problems many of which he then carried for life.

By the late 1890's Jack was regularly publishing short stories and by the turn of the century full blown novels.

By 1904 Jack had married, fathered two children and was now in the process of divorcing. A stint as a reporter on the Russo-Japanese war of 1904 was equal amounts trouble and experience. But that experience was always put to good use in a remarkable output of work.

Twelve years later Jack had amassed a wealth of writings many of which remain world classics. He had a reputation as a social activist and a tireless friend of the workers. And yet on November 22nd 1916 Jack London died in a cottage on his ranch at the age of only 40.

Index Of Contents

Parables don't lie, but liars will parable.
—Lip-King.

Old Long-Beard paused in his narrative, licked his greasy fingers, and wiped them on his naked sides where his one piece of ragged bearskin failed to cover him. Crouched around him, on their hams, were three young men, his grandsons, Deer-Runner, Yellow-Head, and Afraid-of-the-Dark. In appearance they were much the same. Skins of wild animals partly covered them. They were lean and meagre of build, narrow-hipped and crooked-legged, and at the same time deep-chested, with heavy arms and enormous hands. There was much hair on their chests and shoulders, and on the outsides of their arms and legs. Their heads were matted with uncut hair, long locks of which often strayed before their eyes, beady and black and glittering like the eyes of birds. They were narrow between the eyes and broad between the cheeks, while their lower jaws were projecting and massive.

It was a night of clear starlight, and below them, stretching away remotely, lay range on range of forest-covered hills. In the distance the heavens were red from the glow of a volcano. At their backs yawned the black mouth of a cave, out of which, from time to time, blew draughty gusts of wind. Immediately in front of them blazed a fire. At one side, partly devoured, lay the carcass of a bear, with about it, at a respectable distance, several large dogs, shaggy and wolf-like. Beside each man lay his bow and arrows and a huge club. In the cave-mouth a number of rude spears leaned against the rock.

"So that was how we moved from the cave to the tree," old Long-Beard spoke up.

They laughed boisterously, like big children, at recollection of a previous story his words called up. Long-Beard laughed, too, the five-inch bodkin of bone, thrust midway through the cartilage of his nose, leaping and dancing and adding to his ferocious appearance. He did not exactly say the words recorded, but he made animal-like sounds with his mouth that meant the same thing.

"And that is the first I remember of the Sea Valley," Long-Beard went on. "We were a very foolish crowd. We did not know the secret of strength. For, behold, each family lived by itself, and took care of itself. There were thirty families, but we got no strength from one another. We were in fear of each other all the time. No one ever paid visits. In the top of our tree we built a grass house, and on the platform outside was a pile of rocks, which were for the heads of any that might chance to try to visit us. Also, we had our spears and arrows. We never walked under the trees of the other families, either. My brother did, once, under old Boo-oogh's tree, and he got his head broken and that was the end of him.

"Old Boo-oogh was very strong. It was said he could pull a grown man's head right off. I never heard of him doing it, because no man would give him a chance. Father wouldn't. One day, when father was down on the beach, Boo-oogh took after mother. She couldn't run fast, for the day before she had got her leg clawed by a bear when she was up on the mountain gathering berries. So Boo-oogh caught her and carried her up into his tree. Father never got her back. He was afraid. Old Boo-oogh made faces at him.

"But father did not mind. Strong-Arm was another strong man. He was one of the best fishermen. But one day, climbing after sea-gull eggs, he had a fall from the cliff. He was never strong after that. He coughed a great deal, and his shoulders drew near to each other. So father took Strong-Arm's